YOUNG GEORGE AND THE DRAGON

Young George and the Dragon

An Economic Fairy Tale

Paul Justus
with
Linda Joffe Hull

Young George and the Dragon
An Economic Fairy Tale

by
Paul Justus
with
Linda Joffe Hull

ISBN-13: 9780692717813 (Land Share Democracy (L.S.D.) Productions)
ISBN-10: 0692717811
First Edition

Paul Justus
LSD Productions
1725 Grant Street N.E.
Salem, OR 97301
LandShareDemocracy.com

Cover Design by Larry Mansker

To

Andrea, who reveled in the wonder and beauty of Nature

ACKNOWLEDGMENTS

I want to thank all my teachers and friends who introduced me to the ideas underlying this economic fairy tale. I especially want to acknowledge Mason Gaffney who, among many books, wrote *The Corruption of Economics*. It was this book that ultimately persuaded me to attend Council of Georgist Organization conferences.

I would like to profusely thank Linda Joffe Hull for spending countless hours in converting a rather ordinary plot outline into an exciting and lively story. I also thank Mark Graham for introducing me to Linda.

I thank Richard League, posthumously, for expanding my view of the world by introducing me to the idea of psycholinguistic matrices and the connection between inner and outer universes. Richard, also known as Ricardo, taught me many things including the enjoyment of word play and puns. Richard's encouragement to be "better and better" helped prepare me to see the possibility of Land Share Democracy and the importance of acting upon one's convictions.

I probably should thank chroniclers such as Jacobus de Voragine who helped to preserve the story of Saint George and the Dragon in The Golden Legend. I should also apologize to anyone who may be offended for my borrowing this aged fairy tale. It should be noted, however, that a similar story line can be found in ancient Greek Mythology with the tale of Perseus and Andromeda. So, perhaps, this story falls into a long line of literary "borrowing".

I enthusiastically thank Larry Mansker of Eureka Springs, Arkansas for creating and giving me the wonderful cover art for this story. I consider it a masterpiece.

Many thanks go to Ana Ramana for her editing skills and guidance in her poetry retreats.

I thank my late wife, Andrea Radwell, for all the joy of life and love of nature that she shared with me. As a stream ecologist and water mite researcher, she understood the importance of the very small in making life possible for larger organisms, such as us humans. Andrea also understood ecological interconnectedness and that as we protect our Earth's ecological diversity and integrity we increase the possibility of human survival.

Finally, I want to give my thanks in advance to the young readers of this story who see the possibility of moving beyond left and right wing economic ideologies that keep our politicians stuck in political gridlock. I especially want to thank any young readers who unsheathe their scissors of logic and knowledge to implement policies that will create a new political system that approaches an "Economic Holy Grail".

FACING YOUR DRAGON
– Paul Justus

What does it mean to face your dragon:
A metaphor or something true?
And do we call them dragons
because they drag us down?

And when you meet your dragon
on your path,
What will you do?
React with fear and trembling
Or attack with ferocious fearlessness?

After all, would there be great heroes
Without great dragons?
And should you slay your dragon
will you become a dragon too?

Or, perhaps there is another path
An even braver way,
The path of understanding
Where you find some
Magic (love?) to turn

Your dragon into your best friend
So you can hitch a ride
To fly as fast and far
As you wish to go

And even change the world.

ONE

Once upon a time there was a young man named George, George Young, to be exact. George was a clever, resourceful lad of nearly twenty who spent the school year thinking hard as an economics student at the local university and the summers working hard at the local Crown Burger.

One day, as George toiled away in front of the deep fryer, his dark curls plastered to his furrowed brow, he found himself wondering if he was actually thinking harder at work and working harder at school. In Econ class, George lifted little more than a pencil, but somehow seemed to work harder than he ever did flipping burgers, reloading cup dispensers, and filling drive-thru orders at Crown Burger. At school, maybe he was just in over his head, but he couldn't quite make sense of all of the competing economic theories. Particularly those of Karl Krove, his Econ 102 professor, who preached that *Greed is Good* and that government regulation was bad for the economy (or at least the upper one percent elite). Clearly, it was also bad for George who didn't completely buy into Krove's ideology, thus earning him a C for the semester and marring his otherwise straight A average.

"Young George," called his manager, Richard, who was a fan of nicknames, and keeping work as lighthearted as possible. "Time for your fifteen-minute break."

But how did Richard ever feel light when his obligations seemed so heavy? George's minimum wages only earned enough to cover a fraction of his tuition. How did Richard, who earned somewhat more, but had a family to support, ever make ends meet? On his break, George found himself looking at the framed photo of Crown Burger's CEO, Mr. King. The man made 500 times what he did–albeit from a corner office on the top floor of a downtown high-rise, with no plastic booths to wipe down, shake machine to sanitize, or the French fry oil to permeate not only his pores, but his soul. The CEO deserved the financial reward of having started such a successful business, but what about Richard who was committed to The Crown (as he called it), training every new staff member personally and working so late every night, he'd fall asleep at his desk during his lunch break? He wasn't paid nearly what he was worth—especially not after taxes. Should he or anyone be punished for working hard with income and other production taxes?

Somehow, the system felt inequitable.

At the end of his shift, Young George headed to his beaten-up Mustang and was approached by a man carrying a sign claiming he was a homeless veteran. George handed him a dollar and the man graciously thanked him with a *God bless you*. Did giving people handouts really reinforce dependency and laziness like Professor Krove insisted or simply help people in need? George wondered about people in dire poverty who had no way to get ahead. What if this man had no bootstraps to lift himself up? George couldn't possibly support himself on minimum wages after taxes. What hope did the homeless man have? For that matter, what about Richard? Even though he was a man who believed strongly in the power of his own hard work, George always spotted lottery tickets in the office trashcan.

With the doldrums of summer coming to a rapid end, maybe it was time to *supersize* not just burgers and fries, but his thoughts on the subject of taxes on labor, wage inequality, and how best to harness greed. He rushed home, got out of his blue and gold Crown Burger uniform, showered the fryer grease out of his hair, and headed to the Economics department's annual fall meet-and-greet at the Black Dragon Restaurant.

On his way, he spotted none other than Professor Krove, ambling down the block with his gnarled walking stick. As George stopped at the light, Krove entered the crosswalk. For the briefest of seconds, Young George Young fought the impulse to tap him with the car in retribution for the permanent ding on his transcripts. Instead, he took a deep breath and vowed to do the same thing on the academic battlefield.

How he planned to take on Krove, he had no idea, but as he parked and entered the Black Dragon restaurant, he felt energized by the buzz of fellow students and faculty.

"History of Economic Theory should be a decent class," one student said.

"Depending on which professor you get," said another.

"Pot stickers?" a waiter asked, holding a platter.

"Sounds great," George said,

"They're like none you've ever tasted," the first student said as George helped himself to three. "They have some sort of amazing secret ingredient."

More amazing was that raven-haired, blue-eyed Alexis had entered the room. Her beauty had provided a comely distraction from Krove for the hell that was Econ 102. While George had admired Alexis from two rows back the entire spring semester, he'd never actually managed to speak to her.

Miraculously, she looked in his direction.

And then she smiled.

Checking to make sure her attentions weren't directed on someone behind him, Young George Young summoned up his courage to say hello and, hopefully, much more.

Before he could take a single step however, Professor Krove arrived at the party. With his presence, everything–the atmosphere, the casual conversation, even the very air itself changed.

George's courage to approach Alexis vanished in an instant. He began to feel woozy, dizzy even. Conversation seemed to swirl around him, making him feel that much more unbalanced.

A Socialist approach to government is best…

How can an economy work if everyone is on welfare and everyone's honest work is highly taxed…?

I question the need for Almighty Growth. Economic Growth will eventually become Uneconomic Growth with expanding pollution and greater extraction of Earth's natural resources…

Unsure of what was happening or why, George wanted to grab Alexis and clutch onto her for dear life. Instead, he found himself standing beside none other than Krove himself.

A waiter handed the professor a pre-prepared plate of food.

"Young man, would you mind holding my walking stick for a moment while I eat?" Krove asked George.

"I'd be glad to sir," he said, despite feeling otherwise.

"Are you an incoming freshman?" Krove asked, clearly unaware that George had been in his class all semester.

"No, sir." George said, now feeling almost as angry as he was dizzy. "I was in your Econ 102 class this past semester."

"Hmm," Krove sniffed. "Must not have distinguished yourself."

George wanted to argue. He even thought about curling his fist into a ball. He surely would have, had he not felt so downright off.

Instead, he found himself stumbling out toward the restaurant's courtyard for some fresh air.

As he made his way past the lantern lit patio over to the Black Dragon reflecting pool and tried to get his head to stop spinning, a lithe, orange, tabby cat appeared out of nowhere and slipped between his feet.

George tripped and then tumbled directly into the seemingly shallow Koi pond that was anything but. Before he could even register that he needed to get to the edge of the water, he was pulled toward the middle and into a churning vortex.

George was confused and terrified, but somehow amazed that he was still able to breathe, even as he was pulled down, down, down…

Two

Amazingly, George found himself spinning upwards just as quickly as he'd been pulled down and into the vortex. Before he knew it, he'd been catapulted out of the water and deposited in a heap onto the bank of the pond. He tried to figure out what in the world was happening to him, but all he could focus on was how the pond had suddenly morphed into the bluest, calmest body of water he'd ever seen.

Still a little dizzy, and a lot topsy-turvy, he noted that he was surrounded by large, brightly colored flowers and shrubbery. George stood up and leaned against a tree that looked to be an evergreen, but had flaming orange needles.

Somehow, he eventually got his bearings, but unsure what to do next, he decided to follow a road with shimmery copper-hued paving stones.

Where he was going he had no idea, and how far he'd gone even less. Eventually, he spotted a large man wearing a caftan of what appeared to be the same blue and gold stripes as his Crown Burger uniform. As he neared the man, who was downright hulking, he realized that like the flowers and trees, this man was and wasn't familiar. He was, however, sitting cross-legged underneath a fittingly enormous tree with large, purple, heart-shaped leaves. At first, George thought the man was meditating, but soon heard very loud snoring. George wanted to wake him and ask who he was and where they were, but his sheer size was too intimidating.

George decided the best course of action was to tiptoe past instead.

As he did, the man opened one eye and then the other.

"Rats," the man said. "This always happens when I try to meditate."

"It does?" George asked, wondering how many people beside him could possibly have been sucked into a pond, found themselves on the banks of this strange place, traveled down the very same road, and tried to tiptoe past a slumbering giant.

"Every time I sit under the Bodhi tree thinking I'm going to have a productive moment of meditation, I always fall sound asleep."

"Richard?" George asked, realizing the two men shared not only the same clothing color scheme and predilection for catnaps, but similar kind brown eyes.

"I prefer Ricardo," the man said.

"I'm—"

"Young George Young," the man who looked like Richard, but was named Ricardo said with a toothy smile.

"You even know who I am?"

"And I've been waiting for you."

"Why?"

"My job is to help you figure that out."

"What I really need is help getting back to my old world," he said.

"You have work to do here first."

"I do?" George asked, more confused than ever. "Where are we?"

"Shangriland," Ricardo said. "Where everything is a larger, more colorful version of your former reality."

The word *former* echoed through the valley surrounding them.

His old life might not have been much, but at least it was real.

He hoped.

Wondering what had happened, what work he had to do in Shangriland, and a thousand other questions he was suddenly afraid to ask, he simply said, "How did I get here?"

"You expressed a desire to find your True Path," he said. "And now you are here to set upon such a mission."

"You must have the wrong person," George said. "I don't have the vaguest idea where I'm supposed to be headed."

"You are definitely the right person, Young George Young."

"How do you know?"

"Did you not vow to take on the Evil Krove?"

"I do have a professor named Krove who believes that greed is good, which I question, but—?"

"We all have something to accomplish in our lives. We don't always know what that might be, but through our experiences we sometimes find a path that leads to something that is not just good for ourselves, but for society."

"I'm sure Krove is wrong. What I'm not sure about is what I'm doing here, in Shangriland."

"As I said, you are here to seek and find your path," Ricardo said, standing up so tall, George had to crane his neck. "And it is my duty and honor to guide you toward the peace, love, and light that is your destiny."

Despite being that much more befuddled, Young George Young managed to nod.

Starting at that moment, and stretching over the next few hours, days, weeks, or months (George had no idea of time in this place that was now his home), Ricardo did exactly as he'd promised. Much like his doppelganger back at Crown Burger, Ricardo set about teaching him everything he needed to know in order to successfully navigate *The Holy Trail of Life* so he could become a *Knight of the True Path*.

George learned everything from how to use plants for healing, how to exercise one's brain, and the importance of a positive outlook. He learned to respect nature, and if someone needed a helping hand or an act of compassion, it was his job to provide that help. He knew it was his obligation to do no harm. He also learned there were other novices in the Secret order of the True Path, all of whom looked vaguely like his fellow burger flippers.

One morning, after winning a particularly challenging jousting match (a skill he once assumed he'd need to master right behind cave art, Ricardo put his arm around George's shoulder. "You are now ready to start your journey."

"I'm eager for that," George said, looking out toward the horizon. "But I'm still unsure which path I'm to take."

"Follow me," Ricardo said, leading George back to the very Bodhi tree where they'd met. He motioned for him to sit. "Be still, breathe quietly, and let your heart guide you."

George did as he was instructed, sitting as still as possible, focused only on his breathing, and waiting as patiently as possible for some guidance from his heart. But like his mentor and now friend, he must have dozed off, because the next thing he knew, he was waking up, not to any deep insight, but Ricardo standing before him.

"Come," he said. "It's time to celebrate the start of your journey with a farewell feast."

George soon found himself in a large stone meeting house, seated at the head of a banquet table with a roaring fire in the hearth behind him. He stared at a smorgasbord of roasted meats, sweet potatoes, sauerkraut, beans, fresh fruit and dandelion wine, all in colors he never thought possible. George never imagined he would meet, much less break bread with other Knights of the True Path, like Adam, a blacksmith, John Stewart, a miller, and Thomas, a preacher.

And, much like the last party he'd attended, which now seemed like it had been a million years ago and part of a dream in which he lived in the real world, assuming he knew what the real world really was, the conversation began to swirl around him.

The baker may bake his bread out of self-interest, but it also contributes to society so that's a legitimate self-interest because you're getting a quid pro quo…

The bad thing is when somebody takes and doesn't give back…

And what of pollution or any of the other things that could harm other people as the result of production…?

I believe we must find that a system that allows economic freedom, prosperity, fairness, and an ecologically sustainable future for all…

Everyone is equal to their fair stake, but shouldn't the land belong to everyone…?

Ah, yes, the illusive Economic Holy Grail…!

That evening, long after the laughter, conversation, friendship, and feast had died down along with the fire in the hearth, George found himself awake and dizzy with thoughts of his future. He knew his mission would determine his worthiness as a full Knight of the True Path. He knew his journey would be one of self-interest for the sake of good rather than harm. He knew he was to make a difference in the world. He also knew he still had no idea what he was to do to accomplish this goal.

George dozed off for what felt like the briefest of moments before he awoke to the first rays of sunlight.

He got up, dressed, packed his knapsack and made his way from the novice sleeping quarters toward the barn and the sleek, black mustang that was to be his sole companion.

"Ready?" Ricardo said, meeting him there for his send-off.

"Yes," he said, feeling the color rise in his cheeks. "But I still feel confused."

"Close your eyes," Ricardo said, covering George's eyes with his hands. "Now, without giving it any thought, say the first thing that comes into your head."

"Economic," George surprised himself by saying. He then added two more words that he hadn't even thought about since he'd heard them the previous evening. "Holy…Grail."

"Even bigger and better than I expected." Ricardo said, smiling broadly. "You now know exactly what you're searching for."

"The Economic Holy Grail?" George said, repeating the unexpected words that had emerged from his subconscious.

"It's a big job, but I have the perfect tool to assist you in your quest," Ricardo said. He then presented George with a set of very large scissors made of two ten-inch sword-like blades.

"Scissors?" George asked.

"Exlibris," His mentor said with a smile. "One blade is the blade of Knowledge and the other the blade of Logic. Working together, Exlibris creates Wisdom."

"Thank you," George said, tying Exlibris to his knapsack.

"You never know when these blades will come in handy," he said. "But I assure you they will…"

With the gift, and a hug goodbye, George set out on the journey that he prayed would make him worthy of becoming a full Knight in the Order of the True Path.

THREE

Young George Young rode in an uncertain direction for hours or days or weeks. Once again, he wasn't sure of time in Shangriland. He was, however, certain of the intense beauty of his surroundings. Not only were the trees huge, with leaves in colors that made the most spectacular fall seem grim and dull, the grass was a verdant blue. Furthermore, the rivers and streams burbled in clear, magnificent jewel tones. As he traveled along, reveling in the ideal temperatures, the heady fresh air, and the happy chirp of birds, he found himself wondering if the Economic Holy Grail Ricardo and the Knights had spoken of could actually be nature itself. He certainly found himself wishing that this beautiful place was his reality, and that the life he'd lived before he'd gotten sucked down the vortex was the dream.

That was, until one crisp morning.

As he was meandering through a series of lush valleys, he spotted the familiar sight of a green and brown hued forest in the distance. Suddenly compelled, he rushed toward the very spot where the color of the trees and shrubbery changed dramatically. The moment he arrived, however, something far too large to be an insect, or even a bird, suddenly whizzed past his ear.

A second later, he heard the plaintive wail of an injured creature.

"Ha!" echoed the first human voice he'd heard since departing from Ricardo, the other novices, and the True Knights themselves. "Got you!"

Young George Young got down from his horse, tied him to a nearby tree, headed into a nearby forest in the direction of the arrow's path, and came upon a sight he hadn't yet encountered in this world.

The injured creature seemed to be a deer of sorts, but with striped hindquarters like an Okapi or exotic, zebra-striped antelope breed he'd seen at his local zoo. But, unlike any animal he'd ever seen before, the beast had purple and black striped legs and a blue body that almost blended in to his surroundings. In fact, George might not have seen him lying in the brush, were it not for the bright green blood.

A ragged man stepped out from behind a tree holding the bow from which the arrow that stuck out of the animal had come. "Step back or I'll make just as swift work of you."

George stepped backward quickly from a second arrow pointed in his direction.

"I had no choice but slay the beast," the man said, a wild look in his eye. "I'm starving and I cannot afford Draga's fee to hunt in the public commons."

George couldn't help but note that the ragged, sunken-eyed, gaunt man wasn't much older than him. "Draga's fee?"

"Don't toy with me," the man said, increasing the tension in his bowstring. "I mean it."

"I mean you nor anyone else harm," George said. "I swear."

"You weren't sent by the king?"

"I've met no kings since I've been in Shangriland," George said. "Only Ricardo and the Knights of the True Path."

The man seemed to relax, if only slightly. "Knights of the what?"

"I have been sent on a journey to find my true path so that I may be anointed a knight of the order," George said.

"And I'm to believe that?" the man asked with a crazed look that George was unsure whether to attribute to hunger, mental imbalance, or sheer incredulity. "I'll kill you before I'll let you arrest me."

"I have no intention of arresting you," George said, now quite scared, but noting that his adversaries' hands were shaking. "I'm searching for the Economic Holy Grail."

The man laughed aloud. "In the kingdom of Takealot?"

"Is that where we are?" George asked.

"Just outside of it," the man said, pointing to the very forest he'd been riding toward. "Can't you tell?"

"It looks beautiful," George said, having always associated forests in such tones.

"Takealot was once the most beautiful, plentiful kingdom in all of Shangriland," the man said. "Now everything is decrepit, half-dead, or mucky and polluted like the water in the White River."

"What happened?" George asked.

"The Wizard came," the man said.

"The Wizard?" George repeated.

"He put a spell on the king and all the nobles and wormed his way into power," the man said. Seeming to have decided George was no threat, he put down his arms and started toward his catch. "Ever since the wizard began to cast his spells, King Kynon and all his cronies grew richer while the rest of us grow poorer, hungrier, and will soon crumble and die like the plants, animals, and our village itself."

George watched in horror as the man leaned down and began to lap up the green blood.

"Ahh," the man said, his face covered in green blood. "The tonic of life."

George wasn't sure whether he was imagining things, but color seemed to return to the man's face not at all unlike a vampire after a kill.

"I should go," George said, thoroughly unsettled by the giant knife the man then pulled from a sheath at his side.

"Would you like a bite for strength and resolve?" the man asked, slicing into the poor departed creature and pulling out what appeared to be the heart.

"As I said, it's all yours," George said, feeling slightly nauseated by the prospect. "I need to keep moving."

"Good luck with your mission," the man said and took a bite.

George was shaken by his brush with madness as he bid him well, hopped back onto his horse, and headed toward the brown and green forest.

But, just as the man had warned, the grass, trees, and brush though green, were dry. As he proceeded deeper into the forest, the terrain became darker, more desolate, and empty of wildlife. He heard no sign of birds, only the buzz of insects as they stung his neck and arms.

He smelled the stench of what had to be the White River long before he spotted the murky water that ran alongside the village of Takealot.

As he neared the gray, ramshackle town, he already knew there could be no Holy Grail of any kind to be found in such a place.

He was about to turn around before the cobblestones crumbled beneath his horse's hooves and gallop as far away from this place as possible, when a ray of sunshine burst through the clouds and shone down on a turret of the castle.

A lone window filled with sunlight.

Inside he spotted a young woman with raven-colored hair.

"Who is she?" he asked a ragged man heading in his direction.

"One of the only true treasures left in our village," the man said wistfully, but without turning to look. "The King's daughter, Alexis."

FOUR

Georgeknew he was veering from his path by venturing into
the town simply to lay eyes on Alexis.

Alexis.

His heart simultaneously drummed and sunk with the thought
of her name. Everywhere he looked he saw crumbling houses,
boarded-up shops, and sad, tired people. As he entered a bakery
and noted only a few sorry looking loaves of bread in the broken
display case, he wondered how Alexis, his Alexis, could exist in
such a place.

"She doesn't," the baker told him. "The King hasn't allowed
her to venture outside the walls of the castle in forever."

"She was such a dear, kind little girl," said an elderly lady as
George left the bakery, his eyes glued to the window where he'd
spotted her. "I just know she wouldn't let us suffer like this if she
realized what had become of our town."

"And all of our resources," one of the beggars said from the
group of desperate looking souls collecting around him as he sur-
veyed the seemingly impenetrable walls of the castle for a way in.

Seeing as the castle was also surrounded by an inky-looking
moat that was only accessible by a heavily guarded drawbridge,
George wondered how he could get a closer look at Alexis, much
less meet her.

"She hasn't come out of the castle in how long?" he asked.

"Since the wizard came and put her under the same spell as the king and all of the nobles," a little boy said. "He has a stick he waves at whoever shows fear. He also—"

"Shh," his mother said ominously. "Or you'll end up worse off than anyone."

"All of this happened to your town with a wave of his wand?" George asked.

"Because of the wizard, the king put a tax on our homes," said a wizened old man. "Then our businesses…"

"Next, it was everything we bought or sold and on any wages we made…"

"We've all become so poor that most of us have lost our land…"

"And our rents keep going up and up…"

"For those of us who aren't already homeless."

"Now, we can't hunt or collect water from the spring without paying him the fee."

"First, it was our sheep." An old woman shook her head. "Now he wants—"

"Everything is going to the king and the castle, while our lives fall further and further into disrepair."

"Your king sounds downright evil," George said.

"Just gullible and reliant on advisers to alleviate his various fears," a nearby shopkeeper said.

A baby wailed with hunger.

"We'll all die soon if he doesn't lift the fee for hunting in the Commons."

"Not that there's much of any wildlife left," someone said over the murmurs of agreement.

"Nor access to fresh water," the old woman said. "Not with Draga always lurking about looking for payment."

"And this evil wizard is named Draga?" George found himself asking once again.

"No," the little boy said, pointing at the castle, specifically the drawbridge, which had begun to open.

Silence fell over the crowd as the one person George would have gladly left his old life behind simply to avoid appeared on horseback.

"Krove?" George gasped as his nemesis of Econ 102, or a man who looked and carried himself exactly like the dour-faced professor, strode up and stopped beside him.

"Young George Young," he said with a smile that was anything but kind.

"You know who I am?" George asked, fear pulsating through his veins.

"I make it my business to know everything that happens around here," he said, tapping his cane-turned-wand, on George's shoulder. "I also know you are interested in gaining entrance to the castle."

George felt a weird electric tingle course through him, followed by a sense that his resolve was slipping away.

"Come with me," Krove said.

"But my horse…"

"Will be taken care of in the King's stable."

As the drawbridge reopened, George suddenly had no other inclination but to follow the Wizard Krove's lead into the castle.

———◆———

Equally as beautiful as the town was decrepit, the castle gleamed with the finest marble, the most brilliant crystal, and the richest décor George could imagine. Everything shimmered and shined—from the polished wood furniture to King Kynon's jewel-encrusted throne.

And yet, as George was tossed at his feet by a guard, he couldn't help but notice that the otherwise regal King appeared sad.

"What have we here?" the King asked, his brow deeply furrowed.

"This is the young man who was rabble-rousing in the village."

"I wasn't rabble rousing. I was simply wondering–"

"There is nothing to wonder about," Krove said harshly.

"Why are you here?" The King asked.

George stopped himself before he uttered her name. *Alexis.* "I am a seeking the Economic Holy Grail so that I may become a Knight of the True Path."

"The Economic Holy Grail?" the king asked, his voice full of trepidation.

Takealot, with its weak king, Wizard Krove as overload, miserable residents, and crumbling infrastructure would seem to be the furthest George could possibly be from his path. "I had no intention of speaking to anyone in your town about my mission, but they approached me and engaged me in conversation."

"What did they tell you?" he asked.

"Nothing I couldn't see with my own eyes."

"Meaning what?"

George said nothing.

"I command you to say what you are thinking."

"It's just that…" George paused. "Things seem to be out of balance."

"How so?" The king asked.

"Your people are suffering."

"Quite the contrary," Krove said. "They are better able to manage the details of their existence with our help."

"How so?" George asked. "Where's the quid pro quo?"

"This is not good. Not good at all," the King said, wringing his hands. "I fear the people could easily be on the verge of rev—"

"There is nothing to fear," the wizard said, pointing his wand at the king. "Everything is under control."

George watched as King Kynon experienced the same strange electric sensation that had so recently affected his own body. In an instant, the King's expression softened and the tension surrounding him seemed to evaporate. "Everything is under control."

"Exactly," Krove said. "The tolls and fares collected by Draga are due to the vaults as we speak."

"Very good," the King said as the name Draga echoed through the room.

"And the summer wheat harvest will soon fill your grain stores," Krove continued.

Though his eyes were glazed, the King nodded.

"I should lock up our prisoner, right?"

"Yes," the King said. "Lock him up."

"For simply entering your village, listening to what your people have to say, and asking a simple question or two?" Young George Young couldn't help but utter.

"Asking questions is punishable by death," the Wizard Krove said. "Particularly questions that challenge our way of life here in Takealot."

"Death?" George yelped.

"I want to be taken down to the vaults to survey what's come in," the King said, still deep within his trance.

"Your wish is my command, your Lordship," Krove said. "But then we will execute him?"

"Yes," the King said. "As soon as I'm done counting my money."

FIVE

George was tossed into a dark, dank, drafty prison cell with a single, small, barred window. Even worse, his interior view was of Exlibris, still attached to the side of his bag, and hanging by a hook, tauntingly out of reach across the hall from his cell. He tried to calm his racing mind enough to rest, but he couldn't possibly relax any more than he could force down the water or dry bread that had been locked away with him.

Rotting, along with him, while he pondered his imminent demise.

And yet, as he heard the dreaded echo of footfalls coming down the long drafty corridor, his only option was to tamp down his mortal fear. No way George was going to blindly follow Krove straight to the gallows.

Takealot could take everything, but not his life.

Not without a fight.

He shut his eyes and willed away the urge to collapse into a heap on the cold stone floor of his cell.

The footsteps grew louder.

Closer.

They stopped in front of his barred cell.

As he braced himself for a stern voice informing him that his time had now come, all he heard was the rustle of fabric, and, strangely, the meow of a cat.

He dared to open his eyes.

Amazingly, she, ebony-haired, with eyes a deeper blue than he'd ever imagined, and even more beautiful than the girl he'd already fallen half in love with, was standing on the other side of the bars to his cell.

In her arms, she held a plump, orange tabby cat.

"I'm Alexis," she said, staring at him with what seemed to be the utmost curiosity. "The Princess of Takealot."

I know, he didn't say.

"Your Highness," he said with a trembling bow. "I am George Young."

"Hello George Young," she said.

"Why are you here?" he asked, not exactly sure what else to say to her.

"I make it my business to check in on the new prisoners."

"That's very kind of you," he managed, trying not to reveal how incredulous he was that she stood before him, or how weak he felt in the knees.

"It breaks up some of the monotony around here," she said with a shrug. "And gives me someone to talk to besides Aha, my cat."

"I see," he said, his eyes on the cat who seemed to be smiling over the whole interchange. "I appreciate the company."

"What did you do?" she asked, without any further ado.

"Honestly," he said. "I don't know."

"That's what most of the prisoners seem to say."

"I don't doubt that," he said. "If my circumstances are consistent with your laws here in Takealot."

"But you seem very different from the usual sort," she said with the inklings of a smile.

The most dazzling inkling of a smile.

"How so?" George asked.

"Smarter." She paused. "Not as desperate."

He was certainly as desperate as he'd ever been before.

"To be honest…" He dared to look straight into her cobalt eyes. "I saw you in the window of the castle turret and came into town in the hopes of meeting you."

Her cheeks seemed to color. "And got yourself arrested just to get into the castle?"

"It would have been well worth the opportunity, were my life now not on the line."

"What else did you do?" she asked, her voice full of alarm. "Surely there must have been something more."

"I simply came into the village, was greeted by the townspeople, and made the mistake of noting the decrepit condition of the homes, business, common areas, and the poor ragged folks themselves."

"You can't be talking about our village," she said. "It's a lovely place where our subjects are happy and thriving."

"I'm sure it was, your Highness."

"Was?"

"When was the last time you were there?"

A sadness swept across her lovely countenance that somehow marred and multiplied the beauty of her fair skin and delicate features.

"It's been awhile," she finally admitted.

"Since the Wizard Krove came into the court?"

The cat meowed before she could respond and began to bat at the thick black band that kept Alexis' hair at the nape of her neck.

"Aha!" she warned. "Stop it!"

The cat looked more bemused than apologetic.

"My father, the King, assures me the village is still as beautiful and prosperous as ever," Alexis continued.

"But you haven't been down there to see for yourself?"

"I see the tax revenues and the foodstuffs our tax collector takes in exchange for money. Our vault and the larder are overfilled."

"Have you ever asked this tax collector about the condition of the village or its residents?"

"I've never met Draga," she said. "But I am told he is the best tax collector we've ever had."

"Draga, of course." George said. "As a result of this Draga's efficiency, most of the people in the village are starving to death while their businesses shutter and the town crumbles beneath their feet."

"My father would never allow—"

"The Wizard Krove has put a spell on the King, the nobles, and even–"

"Can't be!" she said, seemingly under his spell as well.

"Has your father changed since Krove appeared in the court?"

"My father hasn't been himself since my mother died," Alexis said. "The Wizard is here to make sure the kingdom prospers, which makes my father somewhat happier."

"But not happy?"

"He hasn't been truly happy without mom," she said. "Neither of us have."

"I'm sorry," George said, wishing he could reach out and dry the single tear running down her cheek.

But before George could figure out a way to step close enough, much less try to explain the additional pain the Wizard had wrought upon the kingdom of Takealot, the cat pulled at the hair tie again.

"Aha!" she said again.

As she tried to disengage the cat's paw from her ponytail, the cat leapt into action, somehow tugging the band from her hair, jumping to the ground, dashing through the bars, and into George's cell.

"Come back here!" Alexis pleaded, leaving her to collect the flowing ebony hair which had tumbled to waist length, framing her face and blue eyes.

Rather fetchingly.

But, like every cat George had ever known, the feline did no such thing.

"Please, get her!" Alexis said as the cat seemed to preen as though it had just caught a prized mouse. "I'll be in so much trouble… I'm not allowed to be without my hair tied back in that band…It protects me and…no one but my future husband is supposed to see my hair down like this!"

"No problem," George said, but it turned out to be a problem indeed, as Aha apparently had no intention of letting George anywhere near her.

He moved in one direction and Aha darted in the other, over and over again, until George was thoroughly winded. At which time, the cat froze just out of his reach, smiling. Aha, clearly enjoying the chase, kept up the game until Alexis, frustrated and impatient, grabbed the key to the cell door.

"I'm coming in," she said, holding her hair back as best she could.

"I think you'll have to," George said. "Aha won't let me near her."

"Don't you dare get near me either," she said. "If you do, I will scream bloody murder and the guards will kill you on the spot."

"I would never, ever do anything to hurt you or anyone else," he said. "But especially you."

George would have been embarrassed by both his heartfelt admission and the ease with which Alexis would soon go about collecting her feline, had not the most unusual turn of events occurred. For, as soon as Alexis clicked open the lock and joined him in the cell, Aha darted directly through the bars of the small window that provided the only light or fresh air.

"Aha!" Alexis shouted as the cat landed in the grass and loped across the grounds. "Where are you–?"

"She seems to be headed toward the wall on the other side of the garden," George said.

"This can't be happening," Alexis wailed as the cat looked poised to leap.

Instead, however, the cat stopped abruptly, and looked pointedly at the window.

"Come back, Aha!" Alexis exclaimed. "Now!"

Instead of returning, Aha suddenly disappeared into a hole at the base of the wall.

The next thing George knew, Alexis herself vanished from his cell and was racing across the yard after the cat.

George's hopes of spending whatever little time he had left with the woman of his dreams soon slipped away as Alexis then disappeared behind her cat along into the dark abyss.

While he considered the possibility that alerting the guards to the whereabouts of the princess could be to his advantage with the King, he soon realized that she herself may have provided the key to his freedom.

Indeed, as he rushed over towards the bars of his cell to summon someone to go after her, he discovered that, in her haste, Alexis had not clicked the lock entirely closed.

The next thing he knew, George had retrieved his confiscated backpack, made his way across the lawn, and had slipped into the hole to rescue Aha and Alexis himself.

SIX

U nlike the vortex that had pulled George so quickly and diz-
zyingly into this strange land, the tunnel in which he now
found himself was long, dark, winding, and seemingly endless.
And while Alexis and Aha couldn't be all that far ahead of him, his
voice echoed emptily in the silence.

Consoling himself that his current foray into the unknown
freed him from imminent death, at least at the hands of the Wizard
Krove, he continued to crawl through the inky blackness until, at
long last, he spotted a ray of light up ahead.

"Alexis?" he called as a shadow momentarily blocked the light.

Again, there was no answer.

He finally emerged just outside of the town in the midst of a
field filled with brown, sun-parched crops. The only sign of Alexis
or Aha seemed to be a series of footprints in the dusty ground.

The path led to a marshy area and then disappeared.

Circling the town proper, but not daring to enter for fear
of being recaptured, George spotted a decrepit bridge. As he
approached, he noted that the trees on the other side were fuller
and the grass greener, as in a healthy blue hue. Not only was it
clear that the bridge led to the edge of the kingdom, but the body
of water beneath was anything but murky or dirty like the White
River. In fact, it shone crystal clear like an amethyst in the sunlight.

Half in love with Alexis, but more than halfway to freedom,
George paused for a moment to decide whether to continue his

search for the princess or bolt out of the wasteland known as Takealot as fast as his legs could carry him.

With the clatter of an approaching wagon, he made a third choice by diving into the tall grass along the path. He lay there praying his faded beige clothing blended into these surroundings better than the purple and blue creature he'd watched succumb to the hunter's bow and arrow in the fertile lands beyond the crumbling bridge that was now just out of reach. Willing himself still to keep from rustling the brush surrounding him and giving away his cover, George listened to a few men and some sort of rickety vehicle, as they made their way toward him.

"This corn is the last of my crop," one of the men said. "I have no way to grow any more without adequate water."

"I figured they'd taken ownership of everything they could possibly think of," another said. "But water? We can't survive without water."

"Draga has to accept these textiles as payment," a third man said. "I have nothing else to offer."

"Except for what Draga really wants…"

"Too horrible to even consider…"

"Unless we all want to die, I fear we'll soon have no choice."

As soon as the clatter of wheels on the rocky dirt road passed him by, George dared to peer out toward to the spot alongside the bridge where the men stopped.

"Draga," one of the men shouted.

"We need to fill our vessels," another said.

For a moment, everything from the distant chirp of birds to the myriad insects seemed to grow still.

Suddenly, the pond began to roil.

Though accustomed to expecting the unexpected in this strange land, George's heart began to pound. Instead of the cruel, portly penurious man he'd pictured when he thought of Draga, the surface tension broke and a head appeared from beneath the water.

Far from human, the head was, in fact, that of an enormous black dragon complete with luminescent scales and steely eyes.

Draga bared his teeth. "And what do you have in payment?"

"Corn," one of the men said, shakily. "The very last of my crop."

"Textiles," the second said. "I created them specifically for the King."

Draga looked at the third man with a cold, steely gaze. "And what did you bring?"

"Dried meat from my cellar."

"You may each fill one jug," Draga pronounced with a fiery hiss.

"Only one each?" the first man dared to ask.

"A jug will only last my family a day," said another.

"Then you should have brought me more," Draga said

"This is all we have."

"Not so," the dragon hissed.

"Please, Draga. We must have water to live."

"And you'll have as much of it as you could ever use," Draga said. "Once you pay the unlimited usage fee."

All three men shook their heads.

"That fee is far too precious," one of them said.

The dragon snorted. "One jug of water each."

Heads down, they forked over their hard-earned goods, collected their allotted water, gave forced thanks to the dragon, and started back up the road.

"We have to do something," one of the men said under his breath as they headed past George's hiding place.

"What can we do?" another said.

"The Wizard can't be so greedy as to allow Draga to take our—"

"I sure hope we don't have to find out."

As quiet once again descended around the lake, George was left wondering just what it was Draga could possibly want in exchange for unlimited water usage. He also wondered what he'd demand for crossing the bridge. Was there any way George could make a run for it knowing the Dragon was lurking just below the water's surface? And what of Alexis? How was he to know if she was safe before he did?

His answer came in the form of a meow from the wooded area behind him.

"Aha?" George whispered.

As he dared to look up, the cat scampered in his direction, stopping in the clearing just out of George's reach.

The hair band was still in Aha's mouth.

"Where is the Princess?" he asked the feline.

The cat began to purr as Alexis herself appeared on the crest of the hill.

"Aha!" she said, loping toward the cat.

George was already up and running toward her to pull her toward a stand of trees for cover.

"George?" she exclaimed. "How did you–?"

"I'll explain everything." He grasped her hand. "But it's not safe out in the open."

"Or anywhere else in the kingdom," Alexis said, her voice cracking. "While looking for Aha, I've seen everything you told me about and more. The land is barren, the village is in shambles, and the people…" Tears ran down her cheeks. "Worse even than I could ever have imagined."

"I'm truly sorry to be right," he said.

"And I vow to do whatever it takes to set things right," she said.

Aha appeared and rubbed against her legs.

"You ran me all over creation, you little devil," she said, picking the cat up and removing the hairband from her mouth. "But at least I have this back before I confront my father and the Wizard about what I've seen today."

For reasons he couldn't explain, George's heart sank as Alexis collected the ebony curls and waves that fell past her shoulders and tied her hair back up into a loose bun.

As soon as she did, her face, full of beautiful indignation, seemed to suddenly fall blank.

"Why are we hiding?" she asked.

"Because of Draga."

"Draga..." she repeated

"He is guarding the fresh water supply for the village."

"That is his job," she said, sounding suddenly dazed.

She took a step in the direction of the lake.

"You mustn't," he said. "Draga is not...."

Human, George was about to say, when the water began to roil once again and Draga emerged from underneath the bridge in his full black, scaly, winged glory.

George reflexively put an arm around her and stepped back even further. "You can see how he's terrified the people of Takelot out of almost everything they own." They watched in silent horror as he rose up to his full, black, scaly, winged glory.

"Step back slowly," George said. "I don't think he's seen—"

"I need to go to him," she said, as if in a trance.

"You can't!"

"Have to," she said, stepping forward instead.

George held her back. "He is more fearsome and dangerous than you can imagine."

George felt the heat from Draga's roar of agreement.

"No!" he shouted as Alexis shook off his grasp and ran toward the decrepit bridge.

George chased after her, but just as he was about to reach out and grab her, Aha ran in front of him.

And, once again, he tripped and fell onto the rocky road.

He looked up just in time to see Alexis reach the bridge.

"Alexis…" he managed to shout over the rumble of stones scraping against each other.

Before he could get back onto his feet, a portion of the bridge had given way and Alexis was tumbling toward the water.

Her fall was broken by Draga's outstretched claw.

"Ah, finally," the dragon said, fire billowing from his mouth. "A fair maiden."

SEVEN

"Release her at once!" George commanded, despite the icy terror running through his veins.

Draga did nothing of the sort.

In all of the reading George had done as a boy, he knew dragons could snarl, snore, steal, slink, and even fly off stealthily. The one thing he'd never read of however, was that a dragon could smile.

"The goats and sheep were tasty," the dragon said, positively grinning. "But now that the villagers have finally come to their senses and have sent a maiden as I've requested, they'll enjoy a week's worth of unlimited water."

Horrified as he was that Draga had upped the ante so unthinkably, George prayed that some discourse would delay him from his intended meal long enough to come up with a way to release Alexis from his clawed clutches. "How can you possibly exact such an outrageous cost for a resource the people need for their survival?"

The dragon snorted. "It's my job."

"It's your job to tax your villagers to the point where they are forced to sacrifice their own children as rent for drinking water, a resource that truly belongs to everyone?"

For a moment, the fearsome dragon looked confused, as if no one had ever stopped to question him about the sheer unreasonableness of his demands.

"I'm just doing as I'm told," the dragon said.

"King Kynon told you to take his own daughter on behalf of his subjects?"

Draga's fiery red eyes widened as he glanced down at his intended prey. "You are Princess Alexis?"

Alexis, frozen with fear, could only nod.

"So you see, you must return the princess to the shore safely," George said. "And at once."

Instead of heeding the warning, burning saliva began to dribble from Draga's mouth. "I've heard that princess blood tastes like champagne wrought of the finest honey."

George pulled Exlibris from his satchel and brandished it over his head. "Let her go, I said!"

The dragon roared with smoke-tinged laughter. "You think you can stop me with a big pair of scissors?"

Despite the power and promise he'd felt when Ricardo bestowed Exlibris upon him, George was all too aware that the weapon seemed particularly measly protection against a dragon.

"I—" George managed to utter.

The next thing he knew, there was a whoosh of hot air. A second later, both he and Exlibris had been whisked off the ground and deposited with a clink and a thump onto a prominent chunk of bridge rubble close to shore, but even closer to the creature's reach. Worse, Draga was raising a wide-eyed, petrified Alexis toward his razor sharp teeth.

"Alexis!" George shouted, more in hopes of providing another delay than with any faith that his ploy would work on the catatonic princess. "Command him to let you go! He has to listen to you."

"Must…do…as…we…are…told…" she only uttered.

As hopeless as the situation was, the distraction somehow provided just enough time for another distraction–a band of horseback-clad soldiers who appeared at the top of a nearby hill.

George shuddered when he realized they were led by none other than the equally fearsome Wizard Krove.

With no means of escaping his latest captivity, George's terror gave way to an overwhelming sense of nothing left to lose.

"Wizard Krove!" George shouted, hoping to at least spare Alexis from death's clutches. "Draga has taken the princess hostage. I've tried to tell him who she is and that he has to unhand her, but he doesn't seem to care."

To George's enormous relief, Krove waved his wand.

Draga instantly all but froze in place.

He then bid his men to follow him down to the lake shore.

"You're a brave young lad," Krove said with a wry smile as he arrived. "Not only did you dare to escape the King's prison but have now attempted to take on the mighty, fearsome Draga."

"I was not escaping," George said. "Alexis came to visit me and left the door to my cell open whilst chasing after her cat."

"I see," he said suspiciously. "And why was she chasing her cat?"

"The cat took her hair band."

"The cat did what?" he spat, his eyes narrowing to a glare in the direction of Aha, who was already cowering behind a pile of stones and mortar.

"Alexis was completely distraught," George said. "So when she chased the cat into a hole at the edge of the property I felt that I had to follow."

"To help her get her hair band back?" Krove asked.

"And to make sure she was safe."

"How very gallant of you," Krove said with a yellow-toothed snarl.

"Alexis ran down here to talk with Draga," George said, hoping upon hope that Alexis would emerge from her trance to confirm his story. If she didn't, he stood no chance that Krove might convince the king to spare his life. "The bridge crumbled underneath her feet, the dragon grabbed her, and then me."

"I see that," Krove said.

"Your Wizardship," George dared to say. "I think we can both see that things have become entirely unreasonable."

Even with the water separating them, he could feel the wizard's eyes bore into his very soul. "How so?"

No fear, no fear, no fear, George repeated to himself over and over until he could force himself to speak.

"For one thing," he said in a trembling voice. "The bridge might not have collapsed, exposing Princess Alexis to the will of Draga, had more of the resources collected as tax revenues been put back into the infrastructure of the village."

"The villagers are lazy," Krove said with a dismissive sniff. "If their productivity was anywhere near what it should be, there'd be more than enough funds to repair our weatherworn structures."

"Weatherworn…" Alexis suddenly repeated.

"How can the villagers be productive when they have such little access to the natural resources necessary to produce goods and services?"

"The kingdom oversees farming, livestock production, and the like to stop the people from squandering their resources."

"Squandering…?" Alexis copied, but with question in her voice.

"Only the king and his court appear to be prospering. In the meantime, the crops are dehydrating, the livestock is dying off, the village is decrepit, and the people are hungry, not to mention wage and mortgage slaves without enough access to water, of all things," George said. "Shouldn't the water that is flowing freely beneath the ground be the property of everyone?"

"Nonsense," Krove said.

Alexis began to reach toward her hair.

"Don't!" Krove shouted with what George assumed was misplaced vehemence.

That was, until he lifted his wand in Alexis' direction and pointed it toward the back of her head.

At that moment, George realized what had been bothering him since the moment Alexis had tied her hair back up. "Alexis, he's pointing his wand directly at your hair band!"

"Even more nonsense," Krove said, though his voice was shrill.

"I think he's using the hair band to control your thoughts."

"If you listen to that feeble-minded boy, terrible things will befall you."

"Like she will no longer be under your control?" George asked.

A glimmer seemed to appear in Alexis's eyes.

"Take it off. You have to see if you'll be able to think for yourself ag–"

"Draga," Wizard Krove said. "You may eat the princess."

Alexis gasped.

"Take off the hair band!" George shouted. "Quickly!"

"Eat her," Krove said, pointing his wand at Draga's neck.

"Now!" George shouted.

Thankfully, Alexis seemed come out of her Krove-induced stupor long enough to tug at the hair band.

With the sight of her lovely ebony hair tumbling past her shoulders, the dragon hesitated.

It was then that George realized that Draga's black scales partially concealed a large choker of the same black fabric that Alexis now held in her hand.

"As the princess," she said, her senses immediately coming back just as George suspected, "I command you to—"

"Eat her," Krove interrupted, his wand pointed directly at Draga's neck.

"My father will have both of your heads for this," she said.

Which gave George an idea.

"Eat me instead," he offered.

"What?" all three said in unison.

"I'm offering myself instead of her."

"If that's what you want," Krove smiled wickedly, "I suspect you'll make a delightful appetizer."

"George!" Alexis asked. "What are you doing?"

"If you die, I want to be with you," George said, unable to signal Alexis, even as their eyes met, that he had come up with a plan that was tenuous at best, but was the best chance he could think of to keep them both alive.

"As you wish," Krove said.

"No…!" Alexis cried as the dragon swooped him up.

Little did anyone realize or care, but he'd managed to tuck Exlibris into the back of his trousers.

Never so very close to his fiery, painful demise, George had the smallest chance to save himself, Alexis, and perhaps the lives of many villagers. As the dragon drew George toward his face, the heat of his mouth already singeing his hair and eyebrows, Young George Young pretended to turn away. As he did, he pulled Exlibris from the back of his waistband.

"Krove, you've held an entire kingdom captive with a mere magic wand," he yelled. "And now, I plan to save it with a giant pair of shears."

With that, he snipped the collar from around the neck of the dragon.

EIGHT

For a moment, a horrible stillness fell over the desolate valley. No one, not the birds, insects, nor even the trees dared to breathe until Draga himself took in a deep, loud rattle of a breath.

George, whose eyes were perilously close to the dragon's incisors, couldn't help but notice shades of emerald green along with red and blue colors. The hues, however, were not the result of the dragon's questionable dental hygiene. In fact, the inky, iridescent dragon seemed to be morphing maw to claw from black to shades that were decidedly green with touches of red and blue.

As even his fiery red eyes seemed to cool, the grip of his claws around George loosened and the dragon looked quizzically at both George and Alexis.

Without a word, the dragon set them down safely, gingerly even, on the rocky shore of the lake.

George and Alexis managed to hug, shed a shared tear of joy, and laud each other for their mutual bravery before Krove pointed his wand, albeit shakily, in the direction of his guards.

"Arrest George and the Princess," he commanded. "For treason."

"You will do no such thing," Draga pronounced with a fiery hiss.

In what felt like slow motion, the dragon reached out and knocked the wand from Krove's hand before he could cast a spell on the guards.

Everyone watched in stunned silence as a stream of fire spewed from the dragon's mouth and connected with the end of the wand.

"You tricked me," roared the dragon as the fiery stick flipped end over end and landed in the water with a smoky sizzle. "You said that by wearing the magic choker I'd be immortal, all-powerful, and all my wishes would become reality."

"How was that a trick?" Krove asked. "Haven't you enjoyed all the spoils of the kingdom of Takealot?"

"You brainwashed me by making me wear a choker that turned my soul as dark as my skin," he said. "How was it in mine or anyone else's best interests to tax the already poor villagers until they had nothing to offer but meager crops and sickly goats?" He glanced down at his now mostly green reflection in the surface of the lake. "The water you told me I was protecting is the only valuable commodity left in this desolate, dying kingdom."

"Are you sure about that?" Krove asked. "What greater delicacy is there for a dragon than a delicious maiden?"

"For one thing, I used to be a vegetarian." With a whoosh of surprisingly cool, fresh air, the dragon reached out, snatched Krove from where he stood, and grasped him tightly. "But now, I can't think of anything I'd like more than a meal consisting of the Merchant of Doubt who duped him to instill fear in the hearts of every villager."

While the kindlier, gentler dragon's face was as green as grass after a spring rain, his teeth were no less sharp.

The wizard's high-pitched screech echoed through the valley as the dragon drew Krove closer to his mouth than even George had been.

"Wait!" the wizard shouted as Draga prepared to close his mighty jaws around his head.

"I'm hungry," the dragon responded. "And not just for revenge."

"But if you eat me, the king's spell will never be broken," Krove said.

"Your tricks are simply serving to make me that much more blood thirsty."

"I speak the truth!" Krove pled in a tremulous whisper.

"You haven't spoken a word of truth since you entered this kingdom," the dragon said. "We'll just use that precious wand to undo your spells."

"It's floating in the water, damaged, probably beyond repair," Krove said, his eyes on the wand. "If you want the King back as he was, you'll need my help."

"Save your lies…"

While it was tempting to watch the dragon enjoy everyone's just desserts, bitter though they'd undoubtedly be, what if there was a modicum of truth in what Krove was saying? Much as George loathed the man, he couldn't help but hear the ring of his mentor, Ricardo's voice from somewhere deep inside his head.

Do No Harm…

What if allowing the dragon to gobble him up would, in fact, prevent them from resolving the myriad problems plaguing Takealot?

"Draga," George said. "Please hold up."

"But why?" Alexis asked. "Krove deserves to be punished for all the damage and misery he has brought to the people and the creatures in our kingdom."

Even Krove, now covered in dragon saliva, seemed taken aback that his fate was still under discussion.

"I agree he should be punished, but revenge cannot possibly be the true path," George heard himself saying, the implication of the words sinking in, if only for him. "And what if Krove is telling the truth about the King?"

Draga sniffed. "The King allowed all of this to happen."

41

"I know my father is a fair and just man. He is under the same spell we were or he'd never have allowed Takealot and its subjects to be pillaged in such a horrid manner," Alexis said. "For that reason alone, I ache to see Krove suffer for the crimes he's committed against the kingdom. And yet—"

"You agree with me?" George asked.

"On the off-chance that we do need the Wizard to help bring the King back to his senses, I believe we have to spare Krove," she said. "At least for now."

As their eyes met, George's heart began to pound in a decidedly more positive manner for the first time since he'd been faced with the terrifying, nearly constant adrenaline rush that had been his life in Takealot.

"Thank you, your Highness," George said.

"But I will get to eat him later?" Draga asked, a modicum of hope in his voice. "Won't I?"

"As soon as we are sure the spell has been broken and my father is, once again, himself. You will be rewarded somehow. That, I promise."

Draga emitted a smoky sigh. "I suppose I can just hold onto him here and try not to give into temptation while you go and fetch the King."

"The guards need to take me to the palace," Krove croaked. "The spell has to be broken at exactly the place where I cast it."

The dragon rolled his eyes.

"And I'll need my wand from the lake," Krove said. "Such that it is."

"No way I'm putting you down," Draga said.

"Draga's right," George said. "How do we know he hasn't cast a spell on the guards as well and this is just an escape ploy?"

"Very well," Alexis said. "We will all return to the palace together."

NINE

The King, slumped on his throne, stared so vacantly he didn't even seem to register the dragon's iridescent green with reddish-blue glow. "The dragon collects the taxes and fees. Krove uses the monies to fund the kingdom and the needs of its subjects."

"Believe me, that's not what's happening," Alexis said.

"Weren't we about to start construction on a new viaduct?"

Krove nodded. "Plans were in the—"

"Quiet with your lies!" Draga commanded, giving Krove a warning shake. "You're here to do the business we brought you to do and keep your mouth shut while doing it."

"Why must he keep his mouth shut?" The King looked befuddled. "And what is his business?"

"He is to break the spell he put on you."

The King inspected his arms and then his legs as though looking for any signs of a spell.

"Father," Alexis said. "He changed you from being a benevolent ruler who cared about his kingdom into a dictator who has taxed all of the citizens to the point where they have nothing to offer but–"

"Can't be," the King said, with little to no emotion. "Our coffers are full with the spoils of everyone's labor and productivity. Right Krove?"

"Yes, your High—"

The dragon gave the wizard a more forceful warning shake.

"If I may, your Highness," George said. "I believe—"

"I believe you're the young man I sentenced to death," the King said. "Are you not?"

"George is also the young man who saved my life."

The adoring look Alexis cast in George's direction soothed his once again escalating anxiety about his near and ultimate future.

"Father," Alexis continued. "I was under the same spell as you. We all were, until, well it's a long story, but I chased after Aha, who had left the palace grounds—

"That is forbidden," he said, looking at Krove as if for back-up.

"None of this would have happened it if it weren't for that damn cat," Krove muttered under his breath.

"Nevertheless, I left the door to George's cell open," she said. "He followed to make sure I didn't come to any harm."

"It's a good thing he did," Draga said, nodding in agreement. "Because I, who was also under his greed inspired spell, had every intention of eating your daughter."

"You planned to eat Alexis?" the King asked with a flat affect, but tugging at his jacket as though the information made him physically uncomfortable.

"In payment for the villagers' water rights," Draga said.

The glimmer that seemed to flicker in the King's eyes immediately faltered with the word *rights*. Instead, he gave a brief, non-committal nod. "I see."

"With all due respect," George said. "I fear he doesn't see at all."

"Are you daring to doubt the all-knowing, all-seeing ruler of Takealot?" the King asked.

"The Wizard Krove is a master of deceit who put a spell on everyone in the court including me and you," Draga said, coming to George's defense and giving Krove a stern squeeze as incentive to undo his magic that much faster. "And I, for one, will no longer abide by his trickery."

"Trickery?" the King repeated.

"He needed for all of us to believe that our full vault and coffers meant that the kingdom was growing more and more prosperous, and to keep us from being able to see that we were stealing from our overtaxed, overworked citizens. Worse, we were giving little or nothing back to them in return beyond hopelessness and starvation." Alexis gave an impassioned sigh. "The rampant disrepair of the village, the wildlife surrounding us, and the despair of our people is not only heartbreaking, but life-threatening."

"Invisible Hand," the King muttered.

"More like the Corruptible Hand," Draga snorted, "which he used to stuff his own pocket, then slap the people and resources that make it all possible."

"Greed," the King said, as if by rote. "It is for the ultimate good..."

"Why aren't we getting through to him?" Alexis asked, her voice cracking.

"My wand is too damaged," Krove tinkered with the charred end. "It's not my fault."

"Everything that's happened is your fault," Draga said.

"Maybe things weren't perfect before you arrived, but there was give and take between the castle and the community. Your trickery has destroyed everything and everyone in the Kingdom." A tear rolled down Alexis' lovely cheek. "Even my father is all but gone."

"Krove, you're only alive right now because you said you needed to be in the exact spot where you cast the spell in order to break it without the wand," Draga said. "So break it!"

Krove began to mutter an incantation, first softly, then increasingly louder and in a language George couldn't begin to understand.

Nor could the King, whose eyes remained vacant.

"I'm growing impatient," Draga said. "And hungry."

"I really don't know what's wrong," Krove said, wiping a bead of sweat from his brow.

"Taxes and fees encourage people to work harder," The King looked to the Wizard for approval. "Our prosperity means their prosperity."

"I thought it would work by just merely being here, but I'm afraid the spell can't be broken without the wand," Krove said in response.

"Daddy, you have to listen. The wizard is evil," Alexis beseeched. "He not only imposed taxes on the villagers for everything they grew, produced, created, or bought, but raised rents besides. He took ownership over the public commons, which is now dry and dusty. He gave orders that the White River be polluted and then put a spell on Draga so he'd guard the kingdom's monopoly on the only source of clean water. Even the beautiful wildlife you so admired has been hunted out of hunger and desperation."

"If your people wanted fresh water they had to pay me," Draga added. "And if they wanted to hunt in the wilderness, they had to sneak by me—or die trying."

"Daddy," Alexis said. "When I discovered that everything he'd told us for so long was simply false, his solution was to have me killed off."

"Killed off?" The King repeated.

"Yes, he commanded Draga to eat me."

"I'm ashamed to admit I was seconds away from doing just that," Draga said.

As he watched her silent tears drop onto the golden tiled floor, the King, looking entirely confused, began to pull and tug at his waistcoat once again.

"Your Highness," Krove said. "There's nothing to worry about. Everything is under control."

At that moment, George realized that, in fact, everything actually was under control.

Krove's.

In fact, as the King nodded in agreement, he continued to fuss with his clothing. While he was tugging and shifting, George spotted a flash of very familiar black mesh fabric as he pulled at the buttons running down the placket of his jacket.

It was clear that the Wizard was still up to his usual tricks.

It was also clear that he wouldn't be for much longer because Alexis spotted the same thing at precisely the same moment, and before George could so much as utter the word *trickster*, the Princess burst into sobs.

But not before giving George a look that said, *I've got this,* and motioning Draga to squeeze Krove that much tighter.

Or so George hoped.

"Daddy," she wailed. "I've been so terribly frightened and upset…"

The King, who, thankfully, wasn't entirely immune to the emotional needs of his daughter, opened his arms and motioned her toward him.

"Guards," she asked. "Can we please have a moment to ourselves?"

To George's surprise, the King nodded his agreement. His personal guards made an elaborate turn step and retreated to posts located at doorways on either side of the throne room.

Alexis ran over to the King and collapsed into his arms.

"No!" Krove shouted as she lifted the bottom of her father's jacket, revealing a cummerbund cinched around his waist.

"No mercy for tricksters and liars," George replied, pulling Exlibris from his backpack, running over to join them, and snipping yet another magic yoke, this time from around the King.

"Alexis?" he asked, as she tugged the fabric from around her father and tossed it behind his throne. "What are you doing?"

"Removing Krove's last weapon of control and bringing you back," she said, then reached out to grab George's hand. "We are bringing you back."

For a moment, he simply looked confused yet again, but then, his very essence seemed to change–from his skin which grew instantly less pallid, to his eyes which shone the same clear blue as that of his daughter.

"Daddy, is it you again?"

"I believe so," the King said. "Unfortunately, I've had no idea who I've been or who I've been dealing with."

"Your Highness," Krove said, his voice high and his tone desperate. "You were sad and mourning the death of the Queen, unable to make the tough decisions demanded of a leader. Everything I've done since I arrived in Takealot was for the good of the kingdom and your best interests."

"And you believe it was in my best interests to destroy everything I hold dear, including my daughter?"

"Well, I–"

"You are a liar and a villain of the worst sort," he said. "Who else in my court is wearing or carrying anything made of the same fabric as this brave young man has snipped from off of me?"

As he bid George to make his way around the room and snip the wristbands worn by the palace guards as well as some key members of the court, the King strode over to Krove, who remained firmly in the clutches of the Dragon.

"Hand me that supposedly useless wand of yours," the King commanded.

With no other choice, Krove did as he was told.

A crack echoed through the massive throne room as the King snapped the wand in half against a marble bust in his own likeness.

"What will become of me?" Krove asked in a tremulous, almost childlike voice.

Before the King could answer, the massive double entry doors swung open and a servant came rushing in.

"Your Highness, a group of villagers are at the gates of the castle demanding your audience. I would send them away like always, but they are furious and threatening to revolt."

"Just as I feared all along," the King said.

Silence suddenly filled the room as the King fell deep into thought.

"Please invite them in," he finally said. "Perhaps they should be the ones to address the question of the Wizard's future."

Krove looked that much more concerned.

"If I'm not going to get to eat him, I'm afraid I can no longer hold onto him," the dragon said, smoky drool running down his face. "I simply cannot resist any longer."

"You can't put him down," George said. "Not without risk of him escaping and wreaking more havoc on this or some other unwitting kingdom."

"I think I have a perfect solution," Alexis said with a smile as Aha the Cat, who appeared from behind the throne with the cummerbund in her mouth. "We'll tie him up in his very own chains."

The King left to face the villagers with the instructions that George and Alexis wait with Draga and the merciless but manacled wizard in an anteroom outside the reception hall.

As George listened through an open door, his heart was warmed by the words of the once again regal, reasonable, and rational King.

"It is truly fortuitous that you have come to me on this day," the King said to the small but irate group of villagers. "I intend to hear everything you have to say about what I now know to be dire circumstances of this kingdom."

He remained quiet and patient as the villagers voiced their grievances:

"We wanted to believe that all the changes were for the benefit of Takealot but that's been anything but the case…"

"None of Krove's promises were kept…"

"Even our kids have to work to keep up with all the taxes he's imposed…"

"Given the condition of the school and the lack of funds to pay teachers, it's not as though there'd be much learning going on anyway…"

"But it's no use working harder because we're punished by even higher taxes…"

"The few livestock we still have are starving for lack of grass in the commons where we are forced to corral them."

"We're all growing hungrier by the day…"

"I dream of escaping, but–"

"Draga is always on the prowl," a number of voices finished the sentence in concert.

"Still, people try to sneak out, just to catch something to feed their desperate families."

"Just last week, Thomas Marks was found with antelope. The meat was confiscated and he was killed in the town square as an example."

"We didn't dare to complain, or so much as hint at trying to speak with you, for fear he'd threatened us with more sanctions."

"Or worse."

"I'm truly sorry," The King said at his first opportunity. "For these and all of the other injustices you've suffered."

"Did you not realize what was going on in the kingdom?" someone finally dared to ask.

"Sadly, I had no idea," the King said. "I have just come to find out that he'd placed me and everyone else in the court under a spell that had us all believing that everything was not only fine, but that we were doing the best for the village."

"You couldn't see that the village was falling apart?"

"Or how tattered and hungry we've become?"

"The Wizard's power was so much greater than I ever could have imagined." The King sighed. "Only when the spell was lifted, just today, did I begin to see with any clarity what was happening."

"Your Highness," a man said. "We appreciate your apology, but things have finally reached a level where we no longer–"

"The dragon is demanding one maiden per week for the privilege of survival!" another man interjected. "Even the Wizard can't expect us to submit to giving up something as precious as one of our maidens…"

Murmurs of outraged agreement ricocheted through the room.

"Worse, we fear it has already happened."

"There were screams down by the lake."

"Of that, I am aware," the King said.

"We must insist, for the sake of our daughters and our families, that you do something, immediately."

"I have already taken the first steps," the King said with a nod.

"In light of everything that's happened," one of the seeming leaders of the group said. "I can't help but be a bit–"

"Skeptical?" the King said, turning to nod in the direction of the room where George and company had been waiting. "Behold, my proof."

George pushed the trembling, shackled Wizard into the doorway.

The hush that fell over the shocked crowd quickly gave way to cheers.

"And there's more," the King said.

Draga nudged Krove from behind and emerged behind him.

"Why is the fearsome Draga here?" someone finally stuttered, breaking the stupefied silence his presence caused.

"And why is he green?"

"You need not fear me any longer," Draga said. "Green with shades of red and blue are my natural colors."

"How can that be possible?" one of the men George recognized from down by the lake asked. "Just this afternoon, I heard you demanding a maiden a week so we could have enough water to survive."

"I'm deeply sorry to say that I too was under Krove's spell," Draga said. "But I have been freed and from here on out, I promise to devote the rest of my life to correcting all wrongs I perpetrated upon the Kingdom of Takealot." He shook his massive head. "Many of which I agree were horrible beyond measure."

"Please know that I too suffered at the hands of the Wizard," the King finally added, having allowed the villagers an ample measure of disbelief, surprise, and all-around confusion. "The screams you heard from the lake came from a maiden none other than my very own daughter."

"The princess?" a woman asked incredulously.

"As I've said, I am embarrassed beyond all measure to have demanded any maiden, much less the kind, beautiful, intelligent Princess Alexis," the dragon said, his head hanging low. "But, yes."

"Thankfully, due to the quick thinking of the young man you're about to meet, Alexis escaped unharmed." The King waved both George and Alexis into the room.

Their entrance was met with cheers of joy from the crowd.

The King stepped forward and embraced them both.

"If it weren't for these two and the incredible courage they mustered to break Krove's spell in the face of sure death, all that we once held dear in this kingdom would have surely been lost."

"Kill Krove!" a voice cried out.

"Krove must die!" the crowd began to chant.

George watched the villagers grow increasingly animated while Krove, who hadn't hesitated to order the death of anyone, grew paler than a sheet.

"I can change," Krove cried. "I know tricks that–"

"That you do," the King said.

"You will never change," Draga said. "He can't be trusted."

Cries of *Kill Krove* once again echoed through the room.

"It appears to be the will of the people that you pay for your tricks with a trip to the gallows."

Krove broke down in sobs.

While paying the ultimate punishment for his reign of economic terror seemed that much more imminent than George's death had been, this solution, however logical, continued to leave George as unsettled as when Krove lay in the dragon's claw covered in smoky saliva. Especially when George locked eyes with a terrified boy of about eight, who was cowering behind the the pleats of his mother's full skirt.

"Your Highness," George said. "Could I possibly say something?"

"Please let him, Father,"

"Thank you, Alexis."

Alexis grabbed George's hand. "I know whatever you say will be thoughtful and truly in the best interests of Takealot."

Heeding George's request and his daughter's wishes, the King immediately silenced the crowd. "Seeing as George had the foresight to recognize and free us from the magic bands now restraining Krove, and saved Princess Alexis from paying the ultimate price for uncovering all that was going on in the kingdom, I believe he has earned the right to say his piece before we make a final decision as to the final fate of the source of our misery."

"Thank you," George said, suddenly exhilarated in a way he'd never before felt. "I agree that Krove must pay for his crimes, economic and otherwise, but keep in mind that bloodshed often leads to more bloodshed and eventually a tyranny just like the one you've so recently escaped."

"I still don't see how beheading Krove could be a mistake," a villager said.

"It isn't, necessarily. Before you do, however, I wanted to point out that whether you realize it, or not, you are sharing a moment that rarely happens in the most democratic of societies."

"Democratic?" someone else asked.

"Where I come from, everyone has an equal vote in deciding who governs and what laws take effect. While Takealot is a monarchy, you are blessed to be led by a ruler like King Kynon who has now openly pledged to listen and take into consideration your needs and opinions from here on out."

The King nodded his agreement.

"Perhaps you should consider Krove's defeat as a symbolic beginning," George said. "Maybe, instead of focusing on getting your revenge for all the evil he perpetrated, spend this time telling your King what you need to not only restore the damage done, but working with him to make the kingdom a better place where everyone can thrive in ways they never imagined possible."

"That's what we were promised," an elderly woman sniffed, looking disdainfully at Krove. "When the Wizard first came around."

The crowd became boisterous once again.

"The difference is, you're not putting your trust into an outsider's hands," George continued.

"Ever again," the King said.

"I think hearing from everyone is a brilliant idea," Alexis said. "I, for one, hate to know that children are being made to work when they need to be in school."

"We need schools that aren't falling down in disrepair," a man added.

"Isn't that where our tax money was supposed to go...?"

Soon, everyone seemed to be chiming in.

"We need easy access to fresh water…"

"Enough water so our crops can grow…"

"And grass so we can feed livestock again…"

"How about the ability to leave the kingdom to hunt so we can feed our starving families…?"

"I don't mind taxes if I see them going to fix the crumbling buildings, bridges and–"

"Potholes…Even if I had goods to sell, I can't even get my cart from one end of the village to the other."

"There are so many potholes, so much backbreaking work to do to fix what's broken in this community, where do we even start?"

"What if, instead of killing the Wizard we make him do it?" the little boy who had so recently been hiding behind his mother's skirt asked. "I mean, considering he's magic and all."

As the room erupted in titters and laughter, the King motioned the boy to come forward.

Everyone quickly quieted as he approached.

"I want to hear what you're thinking, lad."

"Well," the boy said nervously. "I was thinking that instead of beheading the Wizard, why don't we make him use his magic to fix all the damage his greed has done to Takealot?"

"Hmmm," the King said. "What is your name, young man?"

"Philip," the boy said.

"And where do you live?"

"We used to have a pretty cottage by the White River."

"Used to?"

"Until it became too polluted and until my daddy went off hunting and never came back."

"And where do you live now?"

The boy whose cheeks were rosy but smudged and whose clothes had seen much better days, looked down. "My mother and I sleep wherever we can, your Highness."

"How would you feel about moving into the wizard's former quarters on the palace grounds?"

The boy's eyes grew huge. "Really?"

"That is, if you will agree to escort me around the village so I can see for myself what has happened and exactly what needs to be done to set things right."

"Wow!" the boy said. "This is like a dream come true."

"More like a nightmare ended," The King said, standing tall and regal once again. "I will spend some time with Philip as my escort, touring the village and all of our lands. When I am done, I will call everyone to assemble in the town square. I will announce my decision about the final fate of Krove and the future of Takealot then."

TEN

George stood beside Alexis. She stood just slightly behind the King. The King stood before his subjects, though not on a lofty balcony looking down on everyone, but rather in the town square itself.

"I called this town meeting to assure each and every one of you that our kingdom will no longer be ruled by the emotions of greed and fear."

Alexis squeezed George's hand.

"After the difficult but truly enlightening events of the last few days, I now realize that we need to address three key issues--Freedom, Fairness, and our Future. In so doing, I hereby decree that each and every individual in Takealot shall hence-forth be the sole owner of himself. Likewise, each individual shall have complete ownership of their labor. And anything that they make with their labor, that is the fruits of their labor, shall also be owned by them."

The villagers broke out in cheers.

"Furthermore," the King added. "All taxes on human pro-duction, including income, sales, wages, and human constructed property, shall be abolished. And no longer will there be a tax drag on the Kingdom!"

"Are you saying you are no longer going to be King?" A man in the front row asked over the incredible din. "Is this is no longer a monarchy?"

"The answer is both yes and no," The King said with a broad smile. "I like to think that for a bird to fly it must balance the action of its left and right wings. Thanks to Princess Alexis, George, and Philip, whom I've asked to stand here with me, and what I've observed touring the village, I believe the way to attain this balance is by converting to a new economic/political system." He paused. "I have named this new system Land Share Democracy."

His words echoed through the town square.

Land Share Democracy.

"Or, if you prefer, *Balance in all Things.*"

"I can't believe this is happening," one of the guards beside Alexis marveled.

"Oh, but it is," Alexis said, her voice full of joy as the King continued.

"I believe the only way to right Takealot's wrongs is to give everybody, not just the royal court, a vote and to allow people who want to help with running the government. The devastating results of Krove's spell, made me realize we must protect economic, social, AND environmental justice. I've also come to see that the real question isn't to share or not to share, but rather what to share."

"With no taxes?" someone shouted.

"That is, if we can all agree the things that come from Nature that go into the production of what people make should naturally belong to the community."

There were nods all around.

"Thus, when a person takes things from the community *commons*, they should pay for what they take. Instead of taxes, rental fees will be collected on the use of all natural resources, including land and water. The revenue will be used to pay for community services, a citizens' dividend or rent security for everyone, and to protect wildlife habitat for ecological services and for the restoration of our Kingdom. This money will, in turn, help citizens pay for the essential natural resources like water." The King paused to give everyone time to take in the depth and breadth of his words. "That is, if all of you are willing to convert to a Land Share Democracy."

"Sounds idyllic," a woman with a far too scrawny baby said.

"It will be," the King said.

"But what are we supposed to do in the meantime?"

"A wonderful question," the King said. "I plan to unlock my vaults and everyone is entitled to a share immediately. The rest will go into a special trust that will provide a monthly dividend for every citizen."

There were not only cheers, but tears of joy throughout the crowd.

"And I think you'll like how we are implementing this and many other changes…"

On the King's cue, the now mostly green Draga appeared on the castle balcony overlooking the square. He was leading none other than Krove by a leash, which attached to a collar made of black mesh fabric.

"I know you've heard the rumors," the King said over the impossibly energized crowd. "Draga, who is naturally docile and this brilliant, beautiful hue was also under the Wizard Krove's spell. The Wizard, however, will never change his colors."

"An eye for an eye!" someone yelled.

"While killing Krove for his wrongdoing seems a fitting punishment, I don't want our first act as a Land Share Democracy to look anything like the dictatorship we've all barely survived." The King responded. "Instead, Krove will spend the remainder of his life in service to our community, starting today. As his first task, he will personally hand each and every one of you a portion of the funds he's spent so much time extracting from your pocketbooks and your very souls."

The townspeople cheered.

"He also has an announcement to make."

"I…" Krove said hesitantly. "It's…It's my…"

Draga gave the clearly reluctant Krove a small shove forward.

"It's my pleasure to announce that in honor of our new system of Land Share Democracy…" Krove seemed to choke trying to get the words out. "The King rechristens the Kingdom of Takealot into the community that will henceforth be known as Sharealot."

Draga emitted a celebratory stream of smoke and fire to commemorate the moment.

"I'm proud of you, Daddy," Alexis said, as the royal trumpeters began to play.

"The richer I got, the more unhappy I became, worrying about my wealth and what was going to happen to it," he said. "I already feel so much lighter and happier."

"Bless you, King Kynon," a frail old woman said, coming up to the edge of the podium. "And bless you, Princess Alexis. I knew you'd come through for us eventually."

"I wish I could take the credit," Alexis said. "If it weren't for George, none of us would be standing here today."

It was at that moment that George spotted a familiar face, not in the crowd, but towering over everyone from the edge of the town square.

"Ricardo!" he said, rushing over to greet not only him, but a contingent of Knights of the True Path.

"Natural resource value must be captured by the public and shared!" George said, by way of greeting as he hugged his dear mentor.

Ricardo grinned. "That, my friend, is–"

"The Economic Holy Grail."

Eleven

"For being the catalyst in the transformation of the Kingdom of Takealot into the community now known as Sharealot, I dub you, Young George Young, a Knight in the Order of the True Path." Ricardo tapped George on each shoulder and atop the head with a ceremonial sword.

As Knight George rose from his knees, accepted the sword, and gazed out upon the village, he couldn't help but breathe in the hope and joy permeating the air, or appreciate all that his own self-interest had made possible.

Especially, and to the delight of everyone, when the fairest maiden of them all leaned in and kissed him.

He closed his eyes to savor the moment…

When he dared open them again, she was still so close, he inhaled her intoxicating floral essence with every breath.

Alexis with her cobalt blue eyes.

Alexis with her raven hair…

Alexis who, suddenly, was no longer wearing either the tiara or any of her regal finery.

In fact, she was wearing jeans and a decidedly modern peasant blouse.

"George?" she asked, concern tinging her sweet, familiar voice. "Princess–?"

She giggled. "It's me, Alexis."

He looked around.

Gone were the newly hopeful villagers, the crumbling brick storefronts ripe for reclamation, or any sign of his fellow Knights of the True Path. "Where am I?"

"The Black Dra–"

"Draga...?"

"Exactly," she said. "You're in the courtyard of The Black Dragon restaurant."

He looked up at the red lanterns hanging in the patio area and the concerned onlookers surrounding him. "What's happening?"

"You slipped and fell into the reflecting pond."

"I did?"

"Do you remember what happened?"

Where did he start?

He forced himself to go back to what felt like years ago, before he'd encountered Ricardo, before his mission to find the Economic Holy Grail, and long before he'd chanced upon the formerly downtrodden Kingdom of Takealot. "Economics department meet-and-greet?"

"Exactly."

"I saw you, ate some pot stickers, and..."

"You were standing with Professor Krove and—"

"Is he still here?" George blurted.

"Of course I am," said a booming voice from the crowd.

George felt slightly faint as Professor Krove, who looked exactly like a wizard in street clothes, appeared from behind Alexis.

"You just slipped and fell a moment ago," he said. "And since you are still so close to the water, I'd thank you if you could reach for my walking stick, which you unceremoniously took when you ran out to the courtyard in the middle of our conversation."

George glanced at the water and spotted Krove's walking stick, or whatever it really was, floating in the center of the pond.

"I'll get it," George said, attempting to sit up.

"Let someone else do it" Alexis said. "You almost drowned."

"I'm fine," he said, looking down at his sopping wet clothing. "There's no reason for anyone else to get soaked too."

The truth was, he wanted to touch the cane, if only to confirms it was mere shellacked, gnarled wood and not something capable of inflicting the damage the alternate universe Krove's wand was capable of causing.

Or was this the alternate universe?

George tried not to think too much as he stepped out into the shallow pond.

"Got it," George said, picking it up to no discernible electrical impulse or otherwise deleterious effect on his body or mind. "But it's cracked, I'm afraid."

"I'd like it back all the same," Krove said, reaching for the cane.

"Of course, Professor Krove," George said, the few sentences they'd exchanged before whatever had happened to George had, well, *happened*. "But before I return your wan...I mean cane, I have something I need to say to you."

"Oh dear," Alexis said. "You definitely must have hit your head when you fell."

"Perhaps so," George said. "Not only was I a student in your class, I sat very near the front of the room, and did my utmost to distinguish myself."

"If you had, I'm certain I'd have known who you were," Krove said.

"Or maybe you didn't want to acknowledge me."

"And why would that be?" Krove asked.

"Because I don't buy your whole Greed is Good philosophy."

"I see." Krove smirked as if expecting his comment all along. "But keep in mind, Greed has driven some of mankind's greatest accomplishments."

"And given rise to a billionaire class that purports to protect Freedom when, in actuality, they distort government, let the "little people" pay the sales and income taxes, and make their income from wage and mortgage slaves."

"Who knew tonight's meal would be served with a moral lesson?" Krove asked.

"And, perhaps, an economic one as well," George said, feeling emboldened, if only by the stick in his hand. "I believe the key to a civil society and a good civilization is striking the right balance or set of balances."

"Do tell," Krove said, dismissively.

"Economic/political systems that allow a privileged few to control and devastate natural resources that Mother Nature made available to ALL condemns the majority of people to live in land-rent servitude, inequality, and impoverishment. Worse, the consequences to our natural environment threaten future generations."

"With that broad a brush stroke, I assume you have a better solution?"

"A more humane and ecological one, anyway."

Krove looked bemused. "Which is?"

"An individual should be the sole owner of himself, his labor and the fruits of his labor. The things that come from Nature that go into the production of what people make should naturally belong to the community." George's heart pounded, but he didn't dare take a breath. "In lieu of taxes on production, a large portion of the rental value of Land should be collected and put into a community trust to pay for essential community services, to protect the ecological balance, and to give all citizens an equal share or dividend to be paid on a monthly basis."

"And you think this will solve all of societies' woes?"

"Maybe it's not utopian, per se, but it's a better way in terms of a political economy."

Krove sniffed. "Next, I suppose you're going to tell me you want to call this new way of thinking Georgism?"

While he knew Krove was being patronizing, he couldn't help but like the sound of it, at least a little. "Actually, I was thinking it should be called Land Share Democracy."

"That knock on the head certainly sent you off to Sharealot, now didn't it?"

George's eyes widened as Krove wrenched the cane from his hand.

"I'll be glad to discuss this further if you have the guts to take my seminar this semester," Krove said. "That is, if you're not afraid."

"Of you?" George asked.

"Or the threat of earning yet another average grade."

"That's much less important than opening my mind to ideas that will benefit society as a whole," George said.

Alexis' expression of admiration and awe screamed Happily Ever After—or at least the definite possibility of a real date in the near future.

"Besides," George said with a smile in her direction. "I have no fear of being average."

———◆———

Dear Reader,

You have come to the end of this story about Young George and his quest for the Economic Holy Grail. However, this may be just the beginning of your personal journey to learn more about Land Share Democracy and similar approaches to economic progress. There are many people and organizations that promote the ideas suggested in this fairy tale.

Join others with the quest to create an economic/political system that promotes greater individual freedom, economic fairness, and an ecologically sustainable future. By working together we can change the world. For more information visit the website: www.InSearchOfTheEconomicHolyGrail.com

ABOUT THE AUTHORS

PAUL JUSTUS is currently working to promote the concept of Land Share Democracy. Paul is an Oregon resident with roots in the Kansas City area. Paul has worked with a variety of organizations that support the tax reform remedy based on the works of Henry George. Paul discovered the importance of Land Economics when he worked in the statistics department of an island kingdom in the South Pacific for the Peace Corps. Paul has worked professionally as a regional planner in Arkansas. He holds a B.A. In Economics from St. Louis University and a Masters degree in Urban Design from the University of Kansas School of Architecture. Please visit his website at www.landsharedemocracy.com

LINDA JOFFE HULL is a freelance editor and the author of THE BIG BANG (Tyrus Books), FROG KISSES (Literary Wanderlust), and three titles in the Mrs. Frugalicious mystery series (Midnight Ink). She is a native of St. Louis, Missouri, but lives in Denver, Colorado. Linda serves on the national board of Mystery Writers of America, is a former president of Rocky Mountain Fiction Writers, and was the 2013 RMFW Writer of the Year. She also holds a B.A. in Economics from UCLA. Please visit her website at www.lindajoffehull.com.

Printed in Great Britain
by Amazon